KB127567

안상학 시선

안상학 시선

Poems by Ahn Sang-Hak

안선재 옮김

Translated by Brother Anthony of Taizé

POET

아시아

차례
Contents

안상학
시선

Poems by Ahn Sang-Hak

POET

벼랑의 나무

숱한 봄
꽃잎 떨궈
깊이도 쟀다
하 많은 가을
마른 잎 날려
가는 곳도 알았다

머리도 풀어헤쳤고
그 어느 손도 다 뿌리쳤으니
사뿐 뛰어내리기만 하면 된다

이제 신발만 벗으면 홀가분할 것이다

Tree on a Cliff

Luxuriant spring.
Petals falling
plumbed the depths
In autumn many
dry leaves flying
knew where to go.

Once you have shaken your locks free,
shaken off every hand,
you need only to jump lightly down.

Now, if you just take your shoes off you'll be lighthearted.

그 사람은 돌아오고
나는 거기 없었네

그때 나는 그 사람을 기다렸어야 했네

노루가 고개를 넘어갈 때 잠시 돌아보듯

꼭 그만큼이라도 거기 서서 기다렸어야 했네

그 때가 밤이었다면 새벽을 기다렸어야 했네

그 시절이 겨울이었다면 봄을 기다렸어야 했네

연어를 기다리는 곰처럼

낙엽이 다 지길 기다려 둥지를 트는 까치처럼

그 사람이 돌아오기를 기다렸어야 했네

해가 진다고 서쪽 벌판 너머로 달려가지 말았어야 했네

새벽이 멀다고 동쪽 강을 건너가지 말았어야 했네

밤을 기다려 향기를 머금는 연꽃처럼

봄을 기다려 자리를 펴는 민들레처럼

그 때 그 곳에서 뿌리 내린 듯 기다렸어야 했네

어둠 속을 쏘다니지 말았어야 했네

그 사람을 찾아 눈 내리는 들판을

헤매 다니지 말았어야 했네

When that Person Came Back
I was Not There

I should have waited for that person then.

Just as a roe deer glances back briefly as it passes a ridge,

I should have stood waiting there for at least that long.

If it was night, I should have waited for dawn.

If the season was winter, I should have waited for spring.

Like a bear waiting for salmon,

like a magpie waiting for dead leaves to fall before building a nest.

I should have waited for that person to come.

I should not have gone racing across the western plains as the sun was setting.

I should not have crossed the eastward river while the dawn was far off.

Like a lotus flower retaining its fragrance, waiting for night.

like a dandelion preparing its bed, waiting for spring.

I should have waited there then, as if putting down

그 사람이 아침처럼 왔을 때 나는 거기 없었네
그 사람이 봄처럼 돌아왔을 때 나는 거기 없었네
아무리 급해도 내일로 갈 수 없고
아무리 미련이 남아도 어제로 돌아갈 수 없네
시간이 가고 오는 것은 내가 할 수 있는 게 아니었네
계절이 오고 가는 것은 내가 할 수 있는 게 아니었네
그때 나는 거기 서서 그 사람을 기다렸어야 했네

그 사람은 돌아오고 나는 거기 없었네

roots.

I should not have gone roaming in the dark.
I should not have gone wandering over the meadows
in falling snow in search of that person.

When that person came like morning, I was not there.
When that person returned like spring, I was not there.
No matter how urgent, I cannot go on to tomorrow,
No matter how reluctant, I cannot go back to yesterday.
The way time comes and goes was not something
possible for me.
The way seasons come and go was not possible for me.
I should have stayed standing there, waiting for that
person.

When that person came back, I was not there.

얼굴

세상 모든 나무와 풀과 꽃은

그 얼굴 말고는 다른 얼굴이 없는 것처럼

늘 그 얼굴에 그 얼굴로 살아가는 것으로 보인다

나는 내 얼굴을 보지 않아도

내 얼굴이 내 얼굴이 아닌 때가 많다는 것을 알고 있다

꽃은 어떤 나비가 와도 그 얼굴에 그 얼굴

나무는 어떤 새가 앉아도 그 얼굴에 그 얼굴

어쩔 때 나는 속없는 얼굴을 굴기도 하고

때로는 어떤 과장된 얼굴을 만들기도 한다

진짜 내 얼굴은 껍질 속에 뼈처럼 숨겨두기 일쑤다

내가 보기에 세상 모든 길짐승, 날짐승, 물짐승도

그저 별 다른 얼굴 없다는 듯

늘 그렇고 그런 얼굴로 씩씩하게 살아가는데

A Face

Just as there is no face other than that face,
all the trees and plants and flowers in the world,
can be seen in that face as living in that face.

Even without seeing my face,
I know there are many occasions when my face is
not my face.

Flowers, no matter what butterfly comes along,
have that face in that face,
trees, no matter what bird comes along, have that
face in that face.

Occasionally I pretend to have a blank face,
sometimes I put on an exaggerated face.
I am inclined to hide my real face like the bones below the skin.

As I see it, while all the world's land creatures, flying
creatures, water creatures

나는, 아니래도 그런 것처럼, 그래도 아닌 것처럼

진짜 내 얼굴을 하지 않을 때가 많다

나는 오늘도

쪼그리고 앉아야만 볼 수 있는 꽃의 얼굴과

아주 오래 아득해야만 볼 수 있는 나무의 얼굴에 눈독

을 들이며

제 얼굴로 사는 법을 배우고 있는 중이다

live bravely with the face they have,

as if saying that they have no other,

I frequently do not show my true face,

like something it's not, not like it is.

So still today,

fixing my eyes on the faces of flowers I have to
crouch down to see

or the faces of trees I can only see far off after a
very long time,

I am engaged in learning how to live with my face.

늦가을

그만하고 가자고
그만 가자고
내 마음 달래고 이끌며
여기까지 왔나 했는데

문득
그 꽃을 생각하니
아직도 그 앞에 쪼그리고 앉은
내가 보이네

Late Autumn

After deciding to stop and give up,
to finally give up,
once I reach home,
comforting and guiding my heart,

Suddenly
I think of that flower,
and see myself
still crouching down before it.

착종

만약에 꽃이 오직 한 마리 벌만 사랑하게 된다면
다른 수많은 벌들을 뿌리치고 기다리거나
그리움의 뿌리를 뽑아 맨발로라도
한사코 찾아다니느라 향기를 잃어버릴지도 모른다

만약에 벌이 한 송이 꽃만 사랑하게 된다면
어찌나 많은 꽃들을 다 모른 체 하고 오직 한 송이에
눌러 앉거나
꽃 진 자리 봉긋한 무덤 앞에 망연자실 푹 무질러 앉아
하 많은 세월을 기다리느라 날개를 잃어버릴지도 모
른다

아마도 인간에서는 향기와 날개의 흔적을 찾을 수 없
는 게 다 그런 전력이 있었기 때문이 아닐까 한다.

Tangles

Suppose a flower were to be in love with just one
single bee,
  rejecting all the many other bees while waiting,
  even uprooting itself in yearning and setting off bare-
foot
  in search of it, perhaps it would end up losing its
scent.

Suppose a bee were to be in love with just one single flower,
  completely ignoring all the many other flowers and
settling on just that one,
  or sitting dumbfounded before the grave covering
the fallen flower
  and waiting on and on, perhaps it would end up losing its wings.

I wonder if that might be the reason why no trace
of scent or wings can be found in human beings.

발밑이라는 곳

내 발밑은 나만의 공간이다
한 날 한 시에 태어난 그 누구라도
서로의 발밑을 동시에 밟을 수는 없다
그런 의미에서 내 발밑은 언제나 나만의 신성불가침
지역이다

사람은 발밑을 밟으면서부터는 단독자다
여섯 살 장마철 처음 밟아 죽인 지렁이
여덟 살 여름날 뭉개버린 개미집
적어도 두 발 아래 학살까지도 책임질 줄 아는 단독자다

흘러간 전쟁 비망록에는 발밑을 빼앗긴 주검들이 많다
가마니 따위를 뒤집어 쓴 시신의 삐져나온 발바닥
그들의 발밑을 유린한 무수한 발자국 소리들은 건재
한가
내가 알기로 전범들의 발밑도 오래지 않아 발바닥에
서 이탈해 갔다

Underfoot

The space that lies beneath my feet is mine alone.
No one born at a given time on a given day
can ever stand on what lies beneath another's feet.
In that sense, what lies beneath my feet is ever a
sacred non-aggression zone, mine alone.

From the time we stand on our own two feet, we become one individual.
The worm first crushed one rainy day when we are six,
the ants' nest crushed when we are eight,
an individual capable of taking responsibility for
such two-footed massacres.

In the memoranda of past wars are many corpses
robbed of their underfoot.
While the soles of corpses' feet stick out from under
straw sacks used to cover them,
does the sound of countless footsteps infringing
their underfoot space continue on?
I have heard that the ground beneath war criminals'

발밑을 가진 적 없는 젖먹이와

발밑을 상실한 노인의 꼼지락거리는 발가락이 닮았다

발밑을 잠시 버리고서야 사랑을 나누는 연인들의 몸짓

발밑 없이 와서 발밑과 동행하다 발밑을 잃고서야 돌
아가는 인생

때가 되면 발밑에 연연하지 않아야 될 때가 한번은 오
는 법이다

누구나 발밑을 밟고 사는 동안은 우선 발밑이 안전하
길 기도한다

발밑은 나눌 수도 공유할 수도 없는 독자적인 것이다

세상 누구의 발밑도 건드려서는 안 된다

많은 부분 나무들에게서 배우고 익힐 필요가 있다

누구의 발밑도 신성불가침 성역이다

feet is soon torn away from the soles of their feet.

The wriggling toes of babes with nothing underfoot are similar
to those of old folk who have lost what was once beneath their feet.
The gesture of lovers making love who have briefly had to give up having their feet on the ground,
a lifetime that comes with nothing underfoot, journeys on with something underfoot, and only returns once what is underfoot is lost.
When the time comes, there's a day when we each have to cease caring about what lies underfoot.

While we live with our feet treading on what lies underfoot, we each pray that it will be kept safe.
Our underfoot space is a personal thing we cannot share with anyone else.
We may not trespass on the space under any other person's feet.
There's a need to learn and master a lot from trees.
The ground beneath each person's feet is sacred ground, sacrosanct.

소풍

내사 두어 평 땅을 둘둘 말아 지게에 지고 간다
새들이 나무를 꼬깃꼬깃 접어 물고 따라 나선다
벗은 이 정도면 됐지
술병을 닮은 위장 속에는 반나마 술이 찰랑이고
파이프를 닮은 허파에는 잎담배가 쟁여져 있으니
무슨 수로 달빛을 밟고 가는 이 길을 마다할 것인가
무슨 수로 햇빛을 밟고 가는 이 길을 저어할 것인가
해와 달이 서로의 빛으로 눈이 먼 이 길을 뒤뚱이며
간다
어느 날은 달의 뒤편에 자리를 펴고 앉아 지구 같은
것이나 생각하며
어느 날은 태양의 뒤편에 전을 펴고 누워
딸내미와 나 같이나 불쌍한 어느 여인을 생각하며
조금씩 술을 비우고 조금씩 아주 조금씩 담배를 당긴다
그때마다 새들은 나무를 펴고 앉아 노래를 부르거나
모래주머니에 챙겨온 콩 두어 개를 꺼내 먹는다
가끔 바람이 불어오고 잊을 만하면 걸어간다

Picnic

I advance with eight square yards of rolled-up ground loaded on my back-pack.

Birds set off behind me, folded trees gripped in their beaks.

They are companions enough.

Inside my liquor-bottle-like stomach, the liquor half filling it sloshes about,

in my tube-like lungs leaf-tobacco is piled high,

so shall I somehow give up this road on which I walk, treading on moonlight?

Shall I somehow dread this road on which I walk, treading on sunlight?

I go staggering along this road where sun and moon are blinded by each other's light.

Some days, sitting on a mat spread on the back of the moon, as I think of earth-like things,

some days, lying on a mat spread on the back of the sun,

thinking of a woman as pitiful as my daughter and myself,

이상하리만치 사랑하는 것들과 가까이 살 수 없는 이
번 생에서 나는 가끔 꿈에서나 이런 소풍을 다녀오곤
하는데 오늘도 그랬으니 한동안은 쓸쓸하지나 않은 듯
툴툴 털고 살아갈 수 있을 것이다

I slowly empty out the liquor, very very slowly tug at the tobacco.

Whenever I do that, the birds unfold the trees, perch there and sing

or take out two beans stored in their gizzards and eat them.

When the wind comes blowing fit to forget, I walk on.

In this current life, unable to live close to what I love stragely I keep going off on picnics and today again, for that reason, I am able to live for a while brushing myself off as if lonesome or not.

내 한 손이 내 한 손을

감기에 걸려 저린 손 살펴보다가 불현듯
언제 한번 내가 내 손을
살갑게 잡아준 적 있었나 생각해보네

없었네 단 한번도
왼손으로 오른손을 곱게 잡아준 적 없었네
갓 태어난 아이의 손을 잡듯 살포시 잡아준 적 없었네
오른손으로 왼손을 정성스레 어루만진 적도 없었네
떨면서 애인의 손을 잡듯 살며시 잡아준 적도 없었네

한 손이 가시 찔렸을 때 맨 먼저 다가가 살피던 한 손
무거운 짐을 들 때 가장 먼저 함께한 손

그 수고로운 손을 서로
추호도 어루만진 적 없었다는 생각에 문득
계면쩍어 하면서 쓰다듬어보네
남의 손인 듯 느껴보네

One of my Hands and the Other

As I examined a hand gone numb from a cold, suddenly,
I reflected: when did I ever clasp affectionately
my hand?

Never. Not once.
I have never clasped daintily my right hand with my
left,
never clasped it gently, as if clasping the hand of a
new-born babe.
And I have never sincerely stroked my left hand
with my right,
have never clasped it nervously as when we trem-
bling clasp a sweetheart's hand.

The hand that first came close and examined the
other when it was pricked by a thorn,
the hand that first of all came to help carry a heavy
bag.

애인의 손인 듯 애무해보네 난생처음

세상에서 가장 사랑스럽게

닿을 듯 말 듯 감싸보네 감싸여도 보네

At the thought that I had never once caressed one hard-working hand

with the other, suddenly,

abashed, I stroke it.

I feel it as if it were someone else's hand.

I fondle it as if it were my sweetheart's hand. For the first time ever,

enclosed and enclosing, barely touching,

as lovingly as ever can be.

팔레스타인 1,300인
-그들은 전사하지 않고 학살당했다

사자가 얼룩말을, 매가 들쥐를 잡아먹듯

개나 소나 잡아먹는 것은 그렇다 치고

먹지도 않는 인간을 인간이 죽이는 것은

자연에서도 거의 볼 수 없는 것이므로 이쯤 되면

자연스럽다는 말은 인간에게서 거두어야 한다

자연스럽지 못한 인간의 역사 앞에서

나는 인간의 무딘 어금니를 증오한다

사자가 얼룩말을 제압하는 것처럼

인간이 인간을 제압할 수 없는 퇴화된 어금니의 역사
에는

다수를 향한 살기를 품은 칼의 발전사가 내장되어 있다

사자 같았다면 최소한 대량학살은 없었을 것이다

명백히 인간이 자행한 칼의 역사다 그러므로

나는 인간의 귀여운 발톱을 증오한다

매가 들쥐를 낚아채 올리는 것처럼

1,300 Palestinians
—They did not die in battle, they were massacred

Although we kill dogs and cows in order to eat them,
as lions kill and eat zebras, as hawks kill and eat
field-mice,
since the way humans kill humans that they will not eat
is something almost never seen in nature, the time has
come
for humans to stop calling it natural.

Faced with humanity's unnatural history,
I detest humans' blunt molars.
In the history of humanity's degenerate molars, hu-
man unable to dominate
human as a lion overpowers a zebra, is included the
history
of the development of the knife, nourishing violent
feelings toward the majority.
If we were like lions, at least there would probably
be no large-scale massacres.
Clearly humanity is the history of the agressive knife.
Therefore,
I detest humans' cute toes.
In the history of humanity's degenerate toes, inca-

35

인간이 인간을 포획할 수 없는 퇴화된 발톱의 역사에는
불특정 다수를 겨냥한 살의를 품은 총의 발전사가 암
장되어 있다
매 같았다면 최소한 무차별 학살은 하지 않았을 것이다
명명백백 인간이 자행한 총의 역사다

자연으로 돌아가자는 말보다 더 낭만적이겠지만
먹지 않으려면 죽이지 마라
사람을 죽여서 먹는 것이 땅이라면 땅을 죽여라
오래된 신화나 낡은 종교나
고리대금의 자본이나 석유 냄새나는 배후나
거대한 제국의 그림자거나 값싼 민족주의거나
혹은 집 없는 설움이거나
사람을 죽여서 얻을 수 있는 상찬은 없다
바이블에서 가르치듯이
네 손에서 하나 되는 것은 죽임이 아니라 평화다
미안하게도 디아스포라는 이제
세계를 떠도는 모든 사람들의 대명사로는 부적절하다
사람을 죽여서 먹는 것이 땅이라면 발 딛고 선 땅을
죽여라

pable of seizing another person

as a hawk grasps and lifts a field-mouse, lies concealed the history

of the development of the gun, nourishing murderous intent toward the unspecified majority.

If we were like hawks, at least we would not commit
indiscriminate slaughter.

Clearly, humanity is the history of the agressive gun.

It might be more romantic than saying that we should
go back to nature,

but there should be no killing if there is no inten-
tion of eating.

If the land means killing people and eating them,
then kill the land.

Whether it be ancient myths or old religions,

usurers' capital or backers stinking of petroleum

or the shadow cast by vast empires or cheap na-
tionalism

or distress at being homeless, there is no praise to
be gained by killing people.

As the Bible teaches,

becoming one in your hands is not death but peace.

Unfortunately the word 'diaspora'

is not appropriate to designate all the people wandering across the world.

If the land means killing people and eating them,

실로 몇 천 년 전 황망한 시온의 꿈으로 돌아가는 것
보다
　차라리 날카로운 어금니를 기르고
　매서운 발톱을 세우는 것이 훨씬 평화에 가깝다

　절망한다, 인간의 역사 속에서 절대 실망시키지 않는
절망
　이마에 총 맞은 팔레스타인 소년의 주검
　상처를 틀어막은 아비의 손을 슴벅슴벅 비집고 나오는
　어린 삶의 무표정한 최후 진술
　어느 때 어디서고 불쑥불쑥 나타나는 절망
　총구를 당기는, 미사일의 단추를 누르는 귀여운 손톱
　학살게임을 하며 미소 짓는 병사의 새하얀 송곳니
　군홧발 속에 가지런한 발톱
　내 몸에도 남아서 총칼의 진보를 인정하고 있는
　그들의 발톱과 송곳니를 닮은 나를 절망한다

　먹지도 않을 인간을 인간이 죽이는 것은 학살이다
　땅을 먹으려거든 땅을 죽이는 것이 마땅하다
　그것이 네 손 안에 하나 되는 평화에 가깝다

kill the land you stand and walk on.

Truly, rather than return to the appalled dreams of Sion of millennia ago,

sharpening blunt molars,

raising fearsome toes would be much closer to peace.

I despair, that despair which never disappoints in human history.

The corpse of a Palestinian boy shot in the forehead,

that young life's last expressionless statement

pushing aside his father's hand that is staunching the wound,

despair suddenly appearing one day somewhere,

cute finger nails aiming a gun, pressing a missile's button,

the white canine teeth of soldiers smiling as they play slaughter games,

the even toenails inside military boots,

that also remain part of my body, similar to their toenails and canine teeth

approving developments in guns and swords, make me despair.

People killing people they will not eat is massacre.

To eat the land, it is right to kill the land.

That is close to the peace in which we become one in your hands.

평화라는 이름의 칼

-엘살바도르의 오스카 로메로 대주교는 정의
가, 마치 뱀처럼, 오직 맨발인 사람들만을 문다는
것을 발견했다. 그는 자기 나라에서 가난한 사람
들은 시초부터, 즉 태어나면서부터 저주받고 공격
받는다는 것을 공개적으로 말했고, 그 때문에 총
을 맞고 죽었다.(에두아르도 갈레아노, 《녹색평론》, 「정
의의 여신은 왜 눈을 감고 있는가?」, 2013년 11-12월호, 14
~15쪽, 김정현 옮김.)

세상에는 외면적인 사람들과 내면적인 사람들이 있
다. 다시 말해서, 세상에는 칼을 밖으로 휘두르는 사람
들과 안으로 들이대는 사람들이 있다는 것이다. 세상은
이 두 부류가 싸우면서 살아가는 공간이다. 평화라는
말의 현실이다.

이런 싸움은 늘 세상이 곧 끝날 것 같은 상황으로 치
닫기 일쑤지만 가까스로 유지되는 까닭도 이들 중 극소
수의 별종들이 있기 때문이다. 한쪽은 밖으로 휘두르던

The Sword Named Peace

—Archbishop Oscar Romero of El Salvador discovered that justice, like a snake, only bites those with bare feet. He publicly stated that the poor in his country were from the outset, that is, from birth, cursed and attacked and he was therefore shot and killed. (Eduardo Galeano: "Why is the Goddess of Justice Blindfolded?" in Green Review, November-December, 2013, p 14-15)

There are external and internal people in the world. In other words, there are people in the world who wield the sword outwardly and people who raise it inwardly. The world is a space where these two kinds of people struggle and live. It is the reality of the word peace.

This kind of struggle seems to be hurtling toward a situation where the world will end soon but as yet the world is barely maintained, because there are only a few of these different kinds. One side refers to those who turn the point of the sword that is swing-

칼끝을 돌려 자신에게 향하는 사람들을 말하고, 또 한 쪽은 안으로 들이대던 칼을 뽑아 밖으로 휘두르는 사람들을 말한다.

그러나 이보다 더 큰 까닭은 정작 따로 있다. 바로, 보이지 않게, 없는 듯 있는 듯 살아가는 부류의 사람들이 있기 때문이다. 평소에는 맨손인 이들인데 어떤 위기 상황이 닥쳐오면 어디서 생겨난 것인지도 모를 칼을 떨쳐들고 나선다. 이들은 대체로 비수를 품고 살았거나 가슴 속에 비수가 있는지도 모르고 살았던 사람들이다. 그냥 두면 죽을 때까지 그렇게 살, 소위 법 없이도 살 사람들이다. (하지만 이들 중 대부분은 자신의 칼을 미처 인식하기도 전에 평화라는 이름의 칼에 의해 학살당했다. 평화를 가장한 평화라는 이름의 칼이 언제나 한 수 빠르기 때문이다.)

이 모든 유형의 사람들은 지금도 끊임없이 재생산되고 있다. 이러한 현상은 엄밀히 말해서, 세상에는, 유사이래로, 온전한 평화가 일순간도 없었고, 또한 앞으로도 무한 지속가능하리라는 불길한 진리를 반증한다. 이것은 또한, 지금도, 도처에서, 터무니없는, 평화라는 이

ing outward toward themselves and the other side refers to those who pull out the sword that is pointing inward and swing it outward.

But actually there is a separate, larger reason. That's because there is a kind of people, unseen, who live somewhere between being and non-being. Normally, they are bare-handed, but when a crisis arises, they advance brandishing a sword that they have produced from somewhere. They are usually people who have either lived keeping a dagger hidden in their breast or have lived not even realizing that there was a dagger hidden in their breast. If you leave them alone, they will live until they die quite without any kind of law. (But most of them were slaughtered by the sword named Peace before they ever knew about their own sword. Because the sword bearing the name of peace, which simulates peace, is always the faster.)

All these types of people are still constantly being reproduced. This phenomenon, strictly speaking, disproves the ominous truth that in the world, there has never, from the very beginning, been a moment of complete peace, and that will continue indefinitely

름의 칼이 끊임없이 확대재생산 되고 있다는 방증이기
도 하다.

　평화로운 세상이란 사람들의 입으로 골고루 밥을 떠
넣는 숟가락 한 자루를 간직하는 것을 최선으로 한다.
정녕 골고루가 힘들면 밥은 차치하고라도 최소한 그 숟
가락 한 자루 정도는 사수하는 것을 차선으로 삼아야
한다. 아무리 힘들더라도 절대, 평화를 가장한, 평화라
는 이름의 칼, 그 칼날에 배식을 맡기는 멍청한 짓은 하
지 말아야 한다. 지금처럼, 칼날로 푼 밥 앞에 입을 벌리
고 있는 작금의 우리들 세상처럼.

in the future. It also shows that still now, everywhere, the sword called Peace is constantly being reproduced at an expanding rate.

The so-called peaceful world is best served by keeping a spoon with which to put food equally into the mouths of people. If doing that equally proves hard to, you have at least to keep that one spoon as a fallback option. No matter how hard it is, we should never be so foolish as to entrust the distribution of food to the sword known as Peace, simulating peace. As our world does now, mouths gaping before rice measured out with a sword blade.

아버지의 검지

지문이 반들반들 닳은
아버지의 검지는 유식했을 것이다
아버지의 신체에서 눈 다음으로
책을 많이 읽었을 것이기 때문이다
아버지가 독서를 할 때
밑줄을 긋듯 길잡이만 한 것이 아니라
점자 읽듯 다음 줄 읽고 있었을 것이다
아버지가 쪽마다 마지막 줄 끝낼 때쯤 검지는
혀에게 들러 책 이야기 들려주고
책장 넘겼을 것이다
언제나 첫줄은 안중에 없고
둘째 줄부터 읽었을 것이다, 검지는
모든 책 모든 쪽 첫줄을 읽은 적 없지만
마지막 여백은 반드시 음미하고 넘어갔을 것이다

유식했을 뿐만 아니라
삿대질 한 번 한 적 없는 아버지의 검지였지만

Father's Forefinger

Father's forefinger, its print worn smooth,
was surely well educated
because it must have read so many books,
following the eyes in Father's body
When Father was reading
it not only served as a guide, underlining the words,
it also read the line below like braille.
Every time Father finished reading the last line on a
page, his forefinger
would pay a visit to his tongue and tell it about the
book
before it turned the page.
It never gave a damn about the first line,
started reading from the second. His forefinger
never read the first line of any page in any book,
then savored the blank margin at the bottom before
turning over.

Not only was it well educated,
Father's forefinger was never shaken at anyone

어디선가 이 시를 읽고는 혀를 끌끌 찰지도 모를 일이다

나는 이렇게 아버지의 여백을 읽고 있는 중이다

but if he gets to read this poem somewhere,
I suppose he might click his tongue.

That is how I am currently reading Father's margins.

아배 생각

뺀질나게 돌아다니며
외박을 밥 먹듯 하던 젊은 날
어쩌다 집에 가면
씻어도 씻어도 가시지 않는 아배 발고랑내 나는 밥상
머리에 앉아
저녁을 먹는 중에도 아배는 아무렇지 않다는 듯
 - 니, 오늘 외박하냐?
 - 아뇨, 올은 집에서 잘 건데요.
 - 그케, 니가 집에서 자는 게 외박 아이라?

집을 자주 비우던 내가
어느 노을 좋은 저녁에 또 집을 나서자
퇴근길에 마주친 아배는
자전거를 한 발로 받쳐 선 채 짐짓 아무렇지도 않다는 듯
 - 야야, 어디 가노?
 - 예……. 바람 좀 쐬려고요.
 - 왜, 집에는 바람이 안 불다?

Remebering Dad

All the time on the move in my youth,
I used to sleep out as often as I took a meal
so that if I came home,
as I sat at the mealtable that stank of Dad's feet
though he washed and washed them,
while we ate he would ask, as if quite unconcerned:
So will you be sleeping out tonight?
No, I'm sleeping here tonight.
But for you, sleeping at home is sleeping out, isn't it?

I often used to stay away from home
and as I was leaving the house one splendidly twilit
evening
I met Dad coming home from work
and as he stood there, supporting his bike with one
leg on the ground, seeming unconcerned:
Hey, are you going somewhere?
Yes.... got to get some air.
Why, don't you get any air at home?

그런 아배도 오래 전에 집을 나서 저기 가신 뒤로는
감감 무소식이다.

Dad left home long ago to go you-know-where and since then I've had no news.

선어대 갈대밭

갈대가 한사코 동으로 누워 있다
겨우내 서풍이 불었다는 증거다

아니다 저건
동으로 가는 바람더러
같이 가자고 같이 가자고
갈대가 머리 풀고 매달린 상처다

아니다 저건
바람이 한사코 같이 가자고 손목을 끌어도
갈대가 제 뿌리 놓지 못한 채
뿌리치고 뿌리친 몸부림이다

모질게도
입춘 바람 다시 불어
누운 갈대를 더 누이고 있다
아니다 저건

Reedbed at Seoneodae

The reeds are resolutely lying toward the east,

showing that all winter long westerly winds blew.

Not so. That is a wound

as the reeds let their hair fly loose and hang free,

urging the eastwardly blowing wind:

Let's go together, let's go together.

Not so. That is a struggle

as the wind urged them resolutely,

let's go together, pulling at their wrists,

and the reeds refused, unable to let go of their roots.

Harshly,

early spring winds came blowing again,

forcing the reeds to lie even lower.

Not so. That was the wind

stroking the reeds' backs as it left.

갈대의 등을 다독이며 떠나가는 바람이다

아니다 저건

어여 가라고 어여 가라고

갈대가 바람의 등을 떠미는 거다

Not so. That was the reeds

pushing at the wind's back

urging it: Go quickly, go quickly.

내 손이 슬퍼 보인다

나는 오늘 내 손이 슬퍼 보인다
개에게 과자를 주려고 손 내밀면
개는 어김없이 뒷발로 서서 앞발을 허우적거린다
그 앞발이 무언가 얻으려고 안달하는 내 손인 듯하여
문득 과자를 든 내 손이 서글퍼 보이는 것이다
좀처럼 꺾이지 않는 직립이 불편하다

사람은 빈손으로 왔다가 빈손으로 간다고 한다
아니다, 사람은 손 없이 왔다가 손 없이 가는 것이다
보라, 기어 다니는 아이까지는 손이 아니라 발이다
똥을 뭉개는 저
기어 다니는 노인의 손도 손이 아니라 발이다
사람은 네 발로 와서 두 손으로 살다가
네 발로 돌아가는 것이다. 그것이 인생이다

두 손으로 사는 동안
잘 난 사람들의 손은 악마적이다

My Hands Look Sad

My hands look sad today.
When I hold out a hand to give the dog a biscuit
the dog invariably stands on its back legs and waves
its front legs.
Those front legs are like my hands when they're im-
patient for something,
so that the hand holding the biscuit looks sad.
Standing upright and rarely bending becomes un-
comfortable.

People say that humans come empty-handed and
leave empty-handed.
It's not so. Humans come without hands and go
without hands.
Look, a baby crawling has no hands, only feet.
That old man crawling about,
rolling in shit, has no hands, only feet.
Humans come four-footed, live two-handed,
then end four-footed again. Such is human life.

While living two-handed,
well-born people's hands are diabolical.
Front feet becoming hands is mainly for possession,

앞발이 손이 되는 것은 대체로 소유를 위해서며
앞발이 손이 되는 것은 대체로 폭력을 위해서며
앞발이 손이 되는 것은 대체로 군림을 위해서다

두 손으로 사는 동안
못 난 사람들의 손은 더 악마적이다
대체로 자본 앞에서 빌어먹기 위해서며
대체로 폭력 앞에서 싹싹 빌기 위해서며
대체로 권력 앞에서 두 손 들기 위해서다

두 손으로 사는 동안 극한에 가서는
악마적인 손과 더 악마적인 손이 부딪친다
빌어먹던 손이 찬탈하여 소유의 손이 되기도 하고,
싹싹 빌던 손이 칼을 빼앗아 들고 살수를 휘두르기도
하고,
항복하던 손이 권력의 숨통을 끊고 군림하기도 한다
두 손의 역사는 끊임없이 싸움을 재생산하는 역사다

나는 오늘
배가 부르면 이내 발로 돌아가는

front feet becoming hands is mainly for violence,
front feet becoming hands is mainly for domination.

While living two-handed,
low-born people's hands are diabolical.
They are mainly used for begging before capital,
they are mainly used for wringing before violence,
they are mainly used for holding up before power.

Driven to breaking point while living two-handed,
diabolical hands and yet more diabolical hands collide.
The hands that once begged now take control and become hands of possession,
the hands that were wrung now take the sword and wield it,
the hands that once surrendered wring power's neck and take control.
Two-handed history is an endlessly repeated history of battle.

Today, as I
consider the hands of the so very meek dog
that withdraws using its feet as soon as it has eaten its fill,
as I consider the hands of the dog that knows nothing of surplus,

저 순하디순한 개의 손을 보면서

도무지 잉여를 모르는 저 개의 손을 보면서

나는 어쩔 수 없이 내 손이 슬퍼 보인다. 그렇지만

개가 두 발로 오래 서 있지 못하는 것은 다행이라 생
각한다

아니래도 손이 자유로운 것이 많아서 어지러운 세상에

개마저 그리 된다면 끔찍하다

과자를 주면

이내 네 발로 돌아가는 저 단순한 동물이

오늘따라 한없이 예쁘게만 보인다. 꼬리를 흔들며

행복한 표정을 짓는 저 개와 섹스라도 하고 싶어진다

그러나 나는 오늘

분명 내 손이 슬퍼 보인다. 빼앗길 것도 없고

빼앗고 싶지도 않는 내 손이 한없이 슬퍼 보이는 것이다

두 손 탈탈 털고 네 발로 기어 다니기에는

이미 세상은 너무나 직립공간인 탓이다

오늘도 일용할 양식을 위해 허우적거리는 내 손이 슬
프다

my own hands cannot help but look sad. Only

I think it fortunate that dogs cannot stay standing for long on their two back feet.

In any case, since hands have so many freedoms, if even dogs

could do that in this crazy world it would be a disaster.

That simple creature that goes back to using four feet

the moment it's given the biscuit,

for today looks infinitely pretty. As it wags its tail

and looks happy, I even feel inclined to have sex with the dog..

But today

my hands look really sad. With nothing to grab,

and not wanting to grab anything, my hands look infinitely sad.

It's because the world is already too much a space for standing upright

for me to get rid of two hands and go crawling about on four feet.

Today, too, my hands are sad, flailing about for my daily bread.

간헐한 사랑

심장이 그러하듯이
일정한 시간 일정한 간격을 두고 되풀이되는 일
살아 있는 모든 것들이 살아가는 방식이지요

퐁퐁 솟는 샘이 그러하듯이
살아 있는 모든 것이 간헐한 법이지요

꽃이 간헐적으로 이 세상에 다녀가듯이
좀 길기는 하지만 우리 사랑도 간헐적으로
이 세상에 다녀가는 것이 아닐는지요
…전생과 이생과 내생… 한 번씩 말이지요

해가 간헐적으로 뜨고 지듯이
달이 간헐적으로 차고 이우듯이
사랑도 간헐적으로 틈틈이 사이사이
쉬었다 이었다 하는 것이 아닐는지요
영원한 것이 있다면 아마도 간헐한 것이 아닐는지요
나는 요즘 언제 있었나 싶은 내 사랑이 간헐하게 이우
는 소리는 들으며 살고 있습니다

Intermittent Love

Repeating itself at regular intervals, regular times,
just like the heart beating,
is the way every living thing lives.

The way a spring comes gurgling out
is the way every living thing is intermittent.

Just as flowers arise then leave this world intermittently,
our love, too, though slightly longer lasting,
arises then leaves this world intemittently, doesn't it?
...a past life, this life, a future life... once each time.

Just as the sun rises then sets intermittently,
just as the moon waxes and wanes intermittently,
isn't love, too, something that pauses then continues,
now and again, on and off intermittently?
If anything is everlasting, perhaps it's what's intermittent.
Nowadays, I live listening to the intermittently fading sound of a love that might once have been.

발에게 베개를

피곤한 발을 베개에 올리고 누웠다가
문득 발이 베개를 베고 누웠다고 생각해본다

가고 싶은 곳에는 경쾌하게 따라오던 발
가기 싫은 곳에는 천근만근 끌려오던 발

오늘 발이 피곤한 것은 아무래도
가기 싫은 곳에 끌려갔다 돌아온 탓이리라
오래된 발톱무좀도
가고 싶은 곳에 못 데려갔거나
가기 싫은 곳에 억지로 끌고 다닌 탓이 크리라 생각한다

발에게 베개를 받쳐주고 누워
머리를 발이라고 생각하며 진짜 발을 바라본다
열 발가락 하나하나 꼽으며 가고 싶은 곳을 헤아려 본다
한 키의 간격을 두고 동거하면서도
그 사이 어디 있는 마음의 발을 자주 동동거리는 바람에

A Pillow for the Feet

Lying down with my tired feet raised on a pillow,
I realize that my feet are lying pillowed on a pillow.

Feet that followed gladly to some place I wanted to go,
feet that were forced to go unwillingly
to some place I did not want to go.

If today my feet are tired, it is because
they were forced to go to some place I did not want
to go.
I think it was very wrong of me
not to take the fungus on my toe-nails where it wanted to go
or to force it to go somewhere it disliked going.

Giving my feet a pillow to support them, I lie down,
and really stare at my feet, imagining my head is my
feet.
As I count my ten toes one by one, I try listing the
places I want to go.

마음의 신발을 찾지 못해 허둥대던 날들을 생각해 본다

더 늦지 않게 마음먹는다

가고 싶은 곳에 앞장서 가는 발을 따라나서리라

머물고 싶은 곳에 발과 함께 머물리라 마음먹어본다

발이 머리가 되고 머리가 발이 되어 생각해본다

머리가 발 같고 발이 머리 같이 살아갈 날을 생각해본다

Although we live together, just one body's length apart,

I think of the days when I was flustered at being unable to find my heart's shoes

as I kept stamping the feet of that heart that lies somewhere in between.

I make up my mind without further delay.

I will follow the feet that lead me where I want to go.

I will stay with my feet where I want to stay.

As feet become head and head becomes feet, I think.

I think of days when head will live with feet, feet with head.

인연

봄꽃 민들레와 가을꽃 쑥부쟁이는 서로 얼굴을 모릅니다
사는 곳이 크게 다르지 않습니다만
아직 한 번도 만난 적이 없습니다
하나는 가을을 모르고 하나는 봄을 모릅니다

한 때나마 마주한 적 있는 당신
가끔 얼굴을 떠올릴 수 있는 것만으로도
쑥부쟁이를 모르는 민들레보다는 마음 가엾긴 합니다만
민들레를 모르는 쑥부쟁이보다는 마음 안쓰럽긴 합니다만

당신은 봄을 지나 여름, 가을, 겨울로 떠나가고
나는 봄을 거슬러 겨울, 가을, 여름으로 떠나온 이후로는
우리가 잠시 스쳤던 계절은 아직 다시 만난 적이 없습

Destined Meeting

Spring's dandelion and autumn's aster know nothing of each other's face.

The places where they live are not very different
but they have never once met.

One knows nothing of spring, the other knows nothing of autumn.

Simply because I have recalled your face now and then
since I met you for a time in the past,

my heart feels sorrier for a dandelion that knows nothing of an aster,

feels more pity for an aster that knows nothing of a dandelion.

You advanced, spring once past, through summer, autumn, winter,

while I went backwards through spring, then winter, autumn, summer,

so we could never meet again after the season

니다만

　민들레와 쑥부쟁이는 아직 서로의 얼굴도 모른다지
않습니까

　그 봄날 그 언덕
　잠시나마 마주서서 나부낀 적 있는 얼굴이여
　내 아직 민들레를 가여워하고
　쑥부쟁이를 안쓰러워하는 걸 보면
　우리가 잠시나마 만난 적이 무척 고맙기는 한가 봅니
다만
　당신이나 나나 그런 봄날 다시 보기는 어려울 것만 같은
　어쩌지 못하는 계절을 굴리며 그냥 이렇게
　생애 끝까지 가야만 하는가보다 생각하는 요즘입니다

when we briefly touched,

   but dandelion and aster know nothing of each other's face, do they?

   Your face, that once fluttered as we faced one another

on that spring day, on that hill!

   When I see how sorry I still feel for a dandelion,

   how much pity I feel for an aster,

   I feel immensely grateful that we met, even just

briefly once.

   While we pass on through the helpless seasons

   and can never see such a spring day again,

   I now feel I have to go on with my life to the end

just like this.

노정

내 걸어온 길 늘 어둠 속이었으나
그래도 여기까지 올 수 있었던 건
그 언젠가 단 한 번 번개 칠 때
잠깐 드러났다 사라진 그 길을 떠올리며
더듬더듬 한발 한발 줄여온 덕분 아니겠는가

남은 길도
캄캄한 길 더듬어 가는 중에
언제고 번개 한 번 더 쳐주길 학수고대하며
그렇게 더듬거리며 가는 길 아니겠는가

Itinerary

The road I have walked so far was always hidden in darkness
and if I was able to come this far it was surely thanks to the way
I was able to shorten the remaining distance, stumbling on step by step
recalling the road that had briefly become visible then vanished again
as lightning flashed just once, one day.

Surely the remaining road, too,
as I go stumbling on along the dark road
eagerly looking forward to another flash of lightning, one day,
will likewise be a road I go stumbling along.

그려본다는 것

모네는
시력을 잃어가면서 새로운 세상을 보았다
만물이 서로의 경계를 지우고
서로를 버리고 서로에게 젖어들어
또 다른 진경을 이루어가는 세상을 그려냈다

에곤 실레는
독감으로 죽은 아내를 그렸다
보이지는 않지만 넉 달도 안 된 뱃속의 아이까지도
그 자신 역시 독감으로 죽어가면서 그려냈다

세상에는 보이지 않아야 보이는 것이 있다
아득하니 볼 수 없을 때야 보이는 것이 있다

Visualizing

As Monet
lost his sight, he perceived a new world.
He painted a world where new realities were emerging,
while everything erased all other boundaries,
things casting each other off, soaking into each
other.

Egon Schiele
painted his wife who died of Spanish influenza.
He painted even the unseen, four-month embryo in
her womb,
while he himself too was dying of flu.

In this world there are things that can only be seen
if they cannot be seen.
There are things that can only be seen when they
are too far off to be seen.

몽골에서 쓴 편지

독수리가 살 수 있는 곳에 독수리가 살고 있었습니다
나도 내가 살 수 있는 곳에 나를 살게 하고 싶었습니다

자작나무가 자꾸만 자작나무다워지는 곳이 있었습니다
나도 내가 자꾸만 나다워지는 곳에 살게 하고 싶었습
니다

내 마음이 자꾸 좋아지는 곳에 나를 살게 하고 싶었습
니다
내가 자꾸만 좋아지는 곳에 나를 살게 하고 싶었습니다

당신이 자꾸만 당신다워지는 시간이 자라는 곳이 있
었습니다
그런 당신을 나는 아무렇지도 아니하게 사랑하고

나도 자꾸만 나다워지는 시간이 자라는 곳에 나를 살
게 하고 싶었습니다

A Letter Written in Mongolia

An eagle was living in a place where eagles can live.
I wanted to be able to live in a place where I could live.

There was a place where birch trees kept becoming more birch-like.
I wanted to be able to live in a place where I could keep becoming more self-like.

I wanted to be able to live in a place where my heart could keep growing better.
I wanted to live in a place where I could keep becoming better.

There was a place where time for you to become more like yourself grew
As I went on loving you without any problem,

I wanted to be able to live in a place where time for me to become more like myself grew.

그런 나를 당신이 아무렇지도 아니하게 사랑하는

내 마음이 자꾸 좋아지는 당신에게 나를 살게 하고 싶
었습니다

당신도 자꾸만 마음이 좋아지는 나에게 살게 하고 싶
었습니다

As you went on loving me without any problem

My heart wanted me to live for you as you kept becoming better.
And you wanted to live for me as my heart kept growing better.

시인노트
Poet's Note

POET

이 세상에 태어나는 모든 슬픔의 출처는 사랑이다.

온전한 사랑이 모습을 잃어가는 꼭 그 만큼의 슬픔이 생겨난다.

모습을 잃어가던 사랑이 완전히 사라지면 슬픔은 완벽하게 태어난다.

내 시는 슬픔이 생겨나는 과정의 기록이자 슬픔을 원래 있던 자리로 되돌리고자 하는 꿈의 현현이다.

The source of all the sorrow born into this world is love.

To the extent that the form of perfect love is lost, sorrow arises.

When love after losing its form disappears completely, sorrow is born perfectly.

My poetry is a record of the process by which sorrow is born and the manifestation of a dream of returning sorrow to its original place.

해설
Commentary

POET

호접몽(蝴蝶夢)¹으로 펼쳐내는 무위자연의 시-학

홍기돈 (문학평론가, 가톨릭대 교수)

안상학의 시 세계는 무위자연(人爲自然)의 인식을 바탕으로 구축되어 있다.² 자연이란 존재하는 것이기에 체(體)를 가지고 있음에 분명하다. 하지만 그 속성은 고정된 형태로 머물러 있는 게 아니라 매 순간 변하는 것이기에 용(用)의 양상으로 드러날 따름이다. 예컨대 태양[陽]이 언제 한 자리에 머무른 적 있었던가. 또한 그 빛은 그림자[陰]를 짓게 마련이다. 만물[相]은 이처럼 조

---

1 나비 꿈. 꿈에서 나비가 되어 즐겁게 놀다가 깬 뒤 장자는 다음과 같이 말했다. "장자가 나비 되는 꿈을 꾸었는지, 나비가 장자 되는 꿈을 꾸는 것인지 알 수 없구나." 이는 각각의 사물이 제각기 독특한 정체성을 가지되, '하나'라는 전체성 안에서 서로 치환 가능해지는 불이성(不二性)의 존재를 가리키는 상징으로 해석된다.

2 무위자연(無爲自然, non-doing naturalism): 자연의 질서에 순응하여 거스르지 않기 위하여 인위를 거부함.

Poetics of Non-Doing Naturalism (無爲自然) Unfolded Through a Dream of a Butterfly[1]

Hong Gi-don (Literary critic)

The world of Ahn Sang-Hak's poetry is built on the philosophy of non-doing naturalism.[2] According to this idea, since nature exists, it clearly has substance (體); however, since its nature is not to stay fixed, but rather to change in every moment, it only appears in variations of itself (用). For instance, the sun never stays in the same position. Also, the sun's light throws a shadow. In the same way, all beings (相) appear,

---

1　This phrase refers to a passage from Zhuangzi, where, awoken after a dream in which he was a happy butterfly, Zhuangzi says: "Now I do not know whether I was then a man dreaming I was a butterfly, or whether I am now a butterfly, dreaming I am a man." It is often interpreted as a symbol of our state in which individual being has its unique identity, and yet becomes interchangeable within the whole.

2　"Non-doing naturalism" means an attitude of rejecting artificiality in order to conform to the order of nature.

화/대립하는 양과 음의 운용을 통해 생겨나고, 변화하고, 소멸한다.[3] 여기서 만물 가운데 한 부류인 인간은 통체(統體)인 자연 안에서 부분자(部分子)로서 위상을 갖는다.[4] 그러니 인간의 존재 의미는 자연의 속성을 체득하는 데서 부여될 터, 이를 가능케 하는 방식이 바로 무위인 것이다.

1. 자연의 용(用)과 생의 형식

자신을 「벼랑의 나무」에 빗대고 있는 시편을 보자. "숱한 봄/ 꽃잎 떨궈/ 깊이도 쟀다// 하 많은 가을/ 마른 잎 날려/ 가는 곳도 알았다"는 1·2연은 음양의 작동

---

3 음양(陰陽, yin-yang): 동아시아 전통사상에서는 모든 사물이 서로 대립되는 속성의 두 측면으로 구성되었다고 파악하였다. 예컨대 천지(天地), 일월(日月), 주야(晝夜), 남녀(男女)와 같은 분류가 이를 드러낸다. 이때 한 측면은 남성적 속성인 양, 다른 한 측면은 여성적 속성인 음에 해당한다. 이는 모든 현상의 발생, 변화, 발전을 설명하는 원리가 되기도 한다. 이러한 사유는 해가 향하는 곳을 양, 등진 곳을 음이라 하는 데서 발전한 것이다.

4 〈통체(統體, whole) - 부분자(部分子, positioner) 세계관〉: 자연은 만물이 출현하고 귀일하는 원천이므로 모든 존재를 아우르는 하나/전체이며, 각각의 만물은 자연의 속성을 담아낸 부분으로서 자연 안에서 상호 관련을 맺으며 나서 자라다가 소멸한다. 이때 인간 또한 부분자로서의 운명에 따르게 된다. 비교컨대 서양 근대철학에서는 우선 개인을 낱낱의 개별자로 설정하고 난 뒤, 각각의 개별자들이 사회계약론에 따라 '사회'라는 합체를 구축한 것으로 설명한다. 이 경우 자연은 개발(인위)이 가해질 대상으로 설정된다. 이러한 인식 체계는 〈개별자(個別子, individual) - 합체(合體, assemblage) 세계관〉이라 정리할 수 있다.

change, and disappear, doing so through the operation of the harmony and antagonism between yin and yang.[3] In this scheme, humans, as just one kind of being among all beings, are a "positioner" in nature as a whole.[4] Therefore, a human being acquires meaning in their existence from learning the attributes of nature—and this is possible through non-doing.

1. The Use (用) of Nature and the Form of Life

Let's take a look at the poem in which the poet compares himself to a "tree on a cliff." Here are the first

---

3   In traditional East Asian thought, all beings are understood to be composed of two opposite aspects, as in phrases like heaven and earth, the sun and the moon, day and night, and men and women. One of these paired concepts is equivalent to yang, a male trait, and the other concept to yin, a female trait. This is also the principle that explains the occurrence, change, and development of all beings. This understanding developed from the time when the direction where the sun rises was called yang and where the sun sets yin.

4   In the Eastern worldview of the "whole (統體)-positioner (部分子)," in the origin from which all beings appear and to which they return, nature is one whole that embraces all beings, and individual beings in it are born, grow in relation to one another, and disappear as a part that bears an aspect of this holistic nature. Like other beings, a human being follows this fate as a "positioner." In comparison to this view, in modern Western philosophy, human beings come first as individuals, and construct the whole as society through contracts among themselves. In this viewpoint, nature is the object onto which individuals can affect development (artificiality). This Western approach can be called a worldview of the "individual (個別子)-assemblage (合體)."

원리를 이제 인지하게 되었다는 진술에 해당한다. 봄은 양의 기운이 약동하는 계절을 나타내며, 가을은 음으로 기울어지는 시점을 상징하므로, 양과 음이 교차하는 시간 속에서 삶의 존재 형식을 깨달았다는 의미로 부각되기 때문이다. 깨달음이 있었다면 깨달은 바를 실행으로 좇기면 하면 된다. 마지막 연 "이제 신발만 벗으면 홀가분할 것이다"가 바로 그 의지를 드러내는 바, 신발을 벗는다는 행위는 인위(人爲)[5]를 부정하고 자연의 운행에 따르겠다는 맥락에서 이해할 수 있다. 절벽을 형상화한 3연의 내용은 깨달음의 절대성에 닿아 있겠다.

자연에서 나왔다가 자연으로 돌아가는 과정이 우리네 삶이라면, 삶이란 어쩌면 「소풍」과 같은 것일지도 모른다. 그런 까닭에 시인은 죽음을 지고 삶을 바라보는 입장에 서 있다. 첫 행 "두어 평 땅을 둘둘 말아 지게에 지고" 간다는 진술이 이를 보여준다. 물론 이 시편에서도 존재를 관통하는 작동 원리는 음양의 교차이다. 해[낮=陽], 달[밤=陰]이 만들어 낸 길을 보라. "해와 달이 서로의 빛으로 눈이 먼 이 길을 뒤뚱이며 간다." 그

5 인위(人爲, artificiality): 자연의 질서를 거슬러 사람의 조작으로 이루어지는 일.

two stanzas: "Luxuriant spring./Petals falling/plumbed the depths//In autumn many/dry leaves flying/knew where to go." They express that the poet espouses the yin-yang operating principle. Spring is the season of waxing yang, while the fall is the season of waning yin. Therefore, these two stanzas indicate that the speaker acknowledges the form of life's being in time, where yang and yin intersect. After this understanding, all one has to do is to put this understanding into practice. The last stanza goes: "Now, if you just take your shoes off you'll be lighthearted." It expresses this will. The act of taking off one's shoes signifies the negation of artificiality[5] and the will to follow nature's flow. The third stanza, which depicts a cliff, touches upon the absoluteness of this realization.

If human life is the process whereby we come from and return to nature, our life could be something like a temporary "picnic." For this reason, the poet is looking at life with death on his back, as the first line of the poem "Picnic" illustrates: "I advance with eight square yards of rolled-up ground loaded on my back-

---

5 Artificiality occurs through human manipulation that is against the natural order.

길을 따라 걷던 시인은 "달의 뒤편"·"태양의 뒤편", 그러니까 삶의 바깥에 자리를 펴고, 마치 나비 꿈을 이야기하는 장자처럼, 이번 생을 떠올려 본다. 이때 새삼 부각되는 것은 "이상하리만치 사랑하는 것들과 가까이 살 수 없는 이번 생"의 애달픈 정조다. 장자가 허방처럼 놓인 현실의 근거를 언급하며 사상가로 나아간 반면, 안상학이 시인으로 자리 잡게 된 까닭은 아마도 이러한 정조에 깊숙하게 침윤하였기 때문일 터이다.

「선어대 갈대밭」은 사물의 대대(待對) 관계를 보여주는 작품이다.[6] 흔히 동쪽으로 누운 갈대를 보면 "서풍이 불었다는" 사실을 유추해 낸다. 갈대의 현황은 바람이 힘을 가한 결과인 까닭이다. 하지만 시인은 이를 바람과 갈대의 관계로 파악한다. 2연 1행의 "아니다"라는 부정이 가능한 까닭은 휘어지는 갈대 줄기의 속성에 주목했기 때문이며, 다시 3연 1행의 "아니다"가 가능해지는 까닭은 땅에 정착한 갈대 뿌리에 주목했기 때문이다. 그렇다면 갈대가 누운 원인의 일단은 갈대 스

---

6 대대(待對): 음·양이 대립한다고는 하나, 각각의 성질이 드러나기 위해서는 서로 상대의 존재가 요청될 수밖에 없다. 가령 밝음이란 어두움을 전제로 했을 때에만 성립 가능한 개념이다. 따라서 대대란 음과 양은 서로 내포하면서 상보 관계로 작동함을 가리키는 용어라 할 수 있다.

pack." In this poem, as well, the operational principle that penetrates all beings is the intersection between yin and yang. To know this, we can look at the road the sun and moon create through their intersecting light: "I go staggering along this road where sun and moon are blinded by each other's light." The poet, who is walking along this road, spreads a mat "on the back of the moon" and "on the back of the sun," that is, outside of life, and thinks of his current life, just like Zhuangzi reflected on his dream of a butterfly. What stands out here is the heartrending sadness of "this current life, unable to live close to what I love most particularly." While Zhuangzi became a philosopher from the understanding of reality as a hollow place, Ahn Sang-hak might have become a poet because of the profound sadness he feels from that reality.

"Reedbed" shows at the same time an antagonistic and a complementary relationship between beings.[6] When we see "reeds... lying toward the east," we deduce that "westerly winds blew." The current state of

6 While yin and yang are antagonistic toward each other, they also need each other to reveal their own natures. For example, light as a concept can be established only when darkness is presupposed. Hence, there exists simultaneously an antagonistic and a complementary relationship between beings.

스로 제공한 셈이 되고 만다. 바람과 갈대의 관계를 통합·정리하는 것이 4연이다. 서로의 상황(속성)을 이해한 듯, 바람은 갈대의 등을 다독이며 떠나고, 갈대는 바람이 쉽게 떠나도록 등을 밀어 준다. 서양 변증법 역시 관계에 주목한다고는 하나, 이는 대립물의 갈등에만 초점을 맞추는 경향이 있다. 바람(이동)과 갈대(정주)가 충돌하는 지점을 드러내되, 서로 감싸는 하나의 관계로 정리한다는 점에서 「선어대 갈대밭」의 사유 방식은 서구 변증법의 논리 구조와 비교할 만하다.

이동과 정주의 관계를 삶/죽음의 층위에서 펼쳐놓은 시편이 「아배 생각」과 「아버지의 검지」다. 아배는 생존하였을 때 집밖으로 나돌기 일쑤인 시인에게 당일의 거처를 묻곤 했다. 형식만 물음일 뿐, 기실 이는 정주하는 아비가 정처 없이 부유하는 아들을 책망하는 내용이다. 하지만 그런 아배도 결국 "오래 전에 집을 나서 저기 가신 뒤에는 감감 무소식이다." 삶이란 게 본디 자연에서 잠깐 소풍 나왔다가 다시 자연으로 돌아가는 과정(이동)인 까닭이다. 정주하는 모든 삶을 끊임없이 이동하는 지평 위에서 파악하는 시인의 견해는 바로 이 지점에서 설득력을 획득하게 된다.

the reeds happened as a result of the blowing wind. However, the poet also understands it as an ongoing interactive relationship between the wind and reeds. The negation "Not so." in the first line of the second stanza is possible because the poet pays attention to the nature of the reed that bends. The same negation is again possible because he notices the roots of the reeds that settle underground. Given these reflections, the reeds themselves offer key reasons for their bending. The fourth stanza integrates and summarizes the relationship between wind and reeds. As if they understood each other's situations (attributes), the wind strokes the backs of the reeds, as it leaves, while the reeds push at the wind's back, helping it to pass quickly. While Western dialectics pay attention to the relationship as well, it focuses on the conflict between two opposites. The mode of thinking in "Reedbed" is in contrast to the logical structure of Western dialectics, since it reveals the point of conflict between the wind (movement) and reeds (settlement) at the same time that it presents a unified relationship in which they embrace each other.

This relationship between movement and settle-

「아버지의 검지」에서는 정주한 자의 세계 인식 방식에 대한 거리 두기가 나타난다. 인간은 고정된[명사형] 언어로써 끊임없이 변화하는[동사형] 자연을 포획하여 사유하는 존재이며, 책은 이를 드러내는 상징이다. 시선이 향하는 대목을 검지가 찬찬히 좇고 있으니, 아버지는 신중하게 책을 읽었을 테다. 그렇지만 언어(책)를 통해 얻는 지식은 늘 모자라거나 넘치는 법이다. 어떤 대목은 지나쳐 버리고, 또 어떤 대목에서는 자신이 생각하는 내용을 덧붙여 메워 넣기 때문이다. "검지는/ 모든 책 모든 쪽 첫줄은 읽은 적 없지만/ 마지막 여백은 반드시 음미하고 넘어갔을 것이다" 그래서 시인은 문자 대신 여백을 읽어 나가기 시작한다. "나는 이렇게 아버지의 여백을 읽고 있는 중이다" 비록 '-것이다'를 반복하며 추측에 머물 수밖에 없지만, 확정된 사실을 지연시키면서 부재하는 아버지에게 다가서는 과정이 아버지 되살리기의 효과적인 방법인 까닭이다. 세계 인식 방편으로도 이는 아마 유효한 바 있을 것이다.

ment is unfolded again, on the level of life and death, in "Remembering Dad" and "Father's Forefinger." The poet's father used to ask the poet, who would often sleep out, where he would sleep, whenever he saw his son. Although this was a question in form, it was in fact the settled father's scolding of his wandering son. However, in the end, "Dad left home long ago to go you-know-where and since then [he has] had no news." This is because life is naturally a process (movement) in which we came from nature to be on a brief picnic, before returning to it. The poet's understanding that all settled lives are on an ever-moving horizon is therefore persuasive.

"Father's Forefinger" also distances itself from the settler's mode of understanding the world. A human is a being that performs thinking by capturing the ever-changing, verb-like nature with fixed, noun-like language. And reading a book is a symbol of this process. Since the father's forefinger slowly followed his eyes, he must have been reading the book carefully. However, knowledge acquired through language (books) always tends to either fall short of or overflow reality. We overlook some parts of the world while read into

2. 정리(情理)의 세계에 펼쳐진 애달픈 사랑[7]

안상학은 존재자의 근거 형식을 살피되 애달픈 정조로 경사한 까닭에 시인이라고 앞서 언급하였다. 『안상학 시선』에 실린 사랑 시편들은 그러한 면모를 보여준다. 「간헐한 사랑」을 보자. '간헐'이란 반복되는 음양의 되풀이 현상을 가리킨다. 심장은 움츠러들었다가 펴지면서 박동을 만든다. 샘은 물을 모은 다음 분출하며, 떠오른 해는 지고, 가득 차오른 달은 이울게 마련이다. 세상의 운행 원리가 그러하니 "영원한 것이 있다면 아마도 간헐한 것이" 아니겠는가. 자, 사랑이 떠나갔다. 사랑이라고 다를 수 있겠는가. "내 사랑이 간헐하게 이우는 소리를 들으며 살고 있습니다." 어찌하지 못한 채 시인은 꺼져가는 사랑을 생의 형식이라 치부하며 그저 안타깝게 용인하고 있는 것이다. 「인연」 역시 마찬가지다. "당신은 봄을 지나 여름, 가을, 겨울로" 떠나갔으니 순리(順理)에 따랐다면, "봄을 거슬러 겨울, 가을, 여름으로 떠나온" 시인은 역리(逆理)를 범한 셈이 된다.[8] 양(⚊)과 음

---

7 정리(情理, reason and sentiment): 인간이 정으로 느끼는 감정적 판단과 이에 따르는 도리.
8 순리(): 순조로운 이치와 도리. 역리(): 살아가는 이치를 거스름. 여기서 이치는 자연의 질서에 해당한다.

other parts: "His forefinger/never read the first line of any page in any book,/then savored the blank margin at the bottom before turning over." Therefore, the poet also begins to read the blank margins instead of the letters: "I am currently reading Father's margins." Although he continues to guess his father's reading and life, he effectively revives his father through the process of approaching his absence by delaying confirmed facts. And this is likely an effective way of understanding the world as well.

2. Heartrendingly Sad Love Unfolded in the World of Reason and Sentiment (情理)[7]

I mentioned above that Ahn Sang-hak is a poet because he tends to approach our fundamental form of being through heartrending sadness. His love poems in this book illustrate this point well. Let's look at "Intermittent Love," for example. "Intermittent" here indicates the repetition of yin and yang. A heart beats by first shrinking, then expanding. A spring gathers water to push it out. The rising sun sets and the full

---

7 "Reason and sentiment" means human sentiment felt through emotions and reason that accompanies it.

(우)이 서로에게 이끌리는 마음은 자연의 이치(理致). 추론하건대, 당신과의 사랑이 싹 텄을 때, 시인은 어떤 이유에서인지 마음이 이끄는 바를 뿌리쳐야 했을 것이다. 그렇게 맞이한 이별 뒤 남는 것은 도저한 아쉬움이다. "당신이나 나나 그런 봄날 다시 보기는 어려울 것만 같은/ 어쩌지 못하는 계절을 굴리며 그냥 이렇게/ 생애 끝까지 살아야 하는가보다 생각하는 요즘입니다"

이별의 상처가 깊숙하게 패인 자는 어떻게든 수습 방안을 찾아야 한다. 「몽골에서 쓴 편지」, 「발에게 베개를」은 그 과정을 보여주는 시편들이다. 독수리는 "독수리가 살 수 있는 곳에" 살며, "자작나무다워지는 곳이" 자작나무의 거처다. 자연의 면모가 그러할진대, 시인은 어찌하여 마음의 흐름을 거부하였던가. 시인이 훼손된 사랑으로 인해 아픈 까닭은 여기서 빚어졌다. 몽골과 한국의 거리는 관계가 훼손된 발신자(시인)와 수신자(당신)의 거리를 연상시키는데, 여하튼 시인은 자신의 뒤늦은 깨달음을 편지에 적어 당신에게 띄운다. "내 마음이 자꾸 좋아지는 당신에게 나를 살게 하고 싶었습니다/ 당신도 자꾸만 마음이 좋아지는 나에게 살게 하고 싶었습니다" 발과 머리의 자리를 바꾸겠다는 「발에게 베

moon is bound to wane. As this is the fundamental law of the universe, as the poet says, "[if] anything is everlasting, perhaps it's what's intermittent." Love also leaves, as it cannot be different from this fundamental law of the universe: "Nowadays, I live listening to the intermittently fading sound of a love that might once have been." Helplessly, the poet embraces his waning love with regret as a form of life.

The same is true of "Destined Meeting." If the poet's object of love followed the law of nature by "[advancing], spring once past, through summer, autumn, winter," the poet must have gone against the law of nature by [going] backward through spring, then winter, autumn, summer." The way yang (♂) is attracted to yin (♀) is the law of nature. It appears that, when love was born between the poet and the object of his love, the poet, for some reason, had to reject this attraction. After this separation, only remarkable regret remains: "While we pass on through the helpless seasons/and can never see such a spring day again,/I now feel I have to go on with my life to the end just like this."

A person with deep wounds from a separation needs to find some way to cope with it. "A Letter Written in

개를」역시 같은 맥락에 놓인다. 분별지(分別智)[9]를 짓는 머리가 아닌, "마음의 발"로서 생의 나침반을 삼겠다는 의지가 주제이기 때문이다. "더 늦지 않게 마음먹는다/ 가고 싶은 곳에 앞장서 가는 발을 따라나서리라/ 머물고 싶은 곳에 발과 함께 머물리라 마음먹어본다" 자, 뒤늦은 깨달음은 과연 파국 상황을 반전시킬 수 있었을까.

쉽지 않은 일이다. 「그 사람은 돌아오고 나는 거기 없었네」를 통해 시인은 토로한다. "시간이 가고 오는 것은 내가 할 수 있는 게 아니었네./ 계절이 오고 가는 것은 내가 할 수 있는 게 아니었네." 어쩌면 "낙엽이 다 지길 기다려 둥지를 트는 까치처럼" 기다리지 못하고 조급하게 서둘다가 일을 망쳤는지도 모를 일이다. "밤을 기다려 향기를 머금는 연꽃"이라든가 "봄을 기다려 자리를 펴는 민들레"가 시인에게 삶의 태도를 조용히 가르치고 있기 때문이다. 사랑이 떠난 자리의 공허가 클수록 사랑의 절대성 또한 더욱 커다랗게 부각된다. 우

---

9 분별지(分別智, discriminating knowledge): 만물이 상호 관계 맺는 양상 속에서 '이것도 저것도(both/ and)' 함께, 즉 양쪽을 아울러 보아야 하는데, '이것이냐 저것이냐(either/or)'를 따지면서 세계를 나누고 가르면서 추구하는 지식.

Mongolia" and "A Pillow for the Feet" show this handling process. An eagle is "living in a place where eagles can live," while "a place where birch trees [keep] becoming more birch-like" is their habitat. As this is the law of nature, why did the poet reject his heart's natural flow? This is why the poet is in pain for his injured love. The distance between Mongolia and Korea reminds us of the distance between the sender of the letter (poet) and its receiver (you), the two people whose relationship was injured. At any rate, the poet sends a letter, in which he writes his belated realization, to the object of his love: "My heart wanted to be able to live for you as you kept becoming better./While you wanted to be able to live for me as my heart kept growing better." "A Pillow for the Feet," which declares the poet's will to switch places between head and feet, deals with the same idea. Its theme is a will to take the "feet" of the heart below rather than head of "discriminating knowledge"[8] above as the poet's guiding principle in life: "I make up my mind without further delay./I will follow the feet that lead me where I want to go./I will

---

8 "Discriminating knowledge (分別智)" is the kind of knowledge that divides the world with "either/or" rather than embracing it as "both/and."

리말에서 "그리다"는 두 가지 의미를 가진다. ① 연필이나 붓 따위로 나타내다 ② 사랑하는 마음으로 간절히 생각하다. 「그려본다는 것」은 그 두 의미를 중첩시키면서 써 내려간 작품이다. "시력을 잃어가면서 새로운 세상을" 본 모네처럼, 시인은 지금여기 자신으로부터 멀리 떨어져 나간 사랑의 존재감을 절박하게 그리고 있다. 「늦가을」임을 아는 데도 "문득" 봄날의 "그 꽃"이 떠오르는 것도 시인이 "그 꽃"을 그리기 때문이며, "언젠가 단 한 번" 내리쳤던 번개를 "언제고 (중략) 한 번 더" 학수고대하는 것도 열렬한 사랑의 순간을 시인이 그리기 때문이다.(「노정」)

여기 "오직 한 마리 벌만" 사랑하여 "한사코 찾아다니느라 향기를" 잃어버린 꽃이 있다. "많은 꽃들을 다 모른 체하고 오직 한 송이에 눌러 앉거나/ 꽃 진 자리 봉긋한 무덤 앞에 망연자실 푹 무질러 앉아/ 하 많은 세월을 기다리느라 날개를" 잃어버린 벌도 있다.(「착종」) 안상학이 하필 애달픈 정조를 노래하는 까닭은 그러한 꽃과 벌처럼 향기·날개를 상실하고 만 탓일 게다. 이로부터 시인의 감각이 열렸다.

stay with my feet where I want to stay." Could this be-lated realization reverse the painful situation?

It is not an easy task. In "When that Person Came Back I Was Not There," the poet says: "The way time comes and goes was not something possible for me./ The way seasons come and go was not possible for me." He could have been ruined because he was rac-ing around hastily rather than waiting patiently "like a magpie waiting for dead leaves to fall before build-ing a nest." It is "a lotus flower retaining its fragrance, waiting for evening" and "a dandelion preparing its bed, waiting for spring" that quietly teach this poet a wise approach to life. The larger the empty space left behind by one's love, the more absolutely that love stands out.

In Korean, the word *geurida* has two different mean-ings: to draw or paint and to sincerely and lovingly miss someone or something. In his poem "Visualizing," these two meanings overlap. Like Monet, who "per-ceived a new world" when he "lost his sight," the poet also desperately depicts the presence of his love that is far away, after leaving him here and now. Even when he knows that it is "late autumn," he also "suddenly...

3. 무위(無爲)의 주체와 인위(人爲)의 폭력성

"도(道)는 그릇이 텅 비어 있는 것 같지만 그것을 써보면 절대로 차고 넘치지 않는다. 심원(深遠)하여 만물의 조종(祖宗)인 듯하다."[10] 『도덕경』 일절인데, 여기서 도는 자연을 가리킨다. 자연의 체[體]는 비어 있으므로 매 순간 변화 가능하며, 만물을 품어 길러낼 수 있는 것이다. 주지하다시피 근대적 주체는 끊임없이 욕망을 충족시키면서 비대해져 가는 면모를 특징으로 한다. 자연의 속성을 체득하기 위하여 근대적 주체와는 다른 주체를 구성해야 하는 이유가 여기 있다. 그래서 시인은 주체가 온전하게 소유할 수 있는 영역을 한정하여 제시해 놓았다. 시 「발밑이라는 곳」을 보자. "내 발밑은 나만의 공간이다./ 한 날 한 시에 태어난 그 누구라도/ 서로의 발밑을 동시에 밟을 수는 없다" 딛고 선 발밑에 대한 소유는 제한되는데, "발밑 없이 와서" 종국엔 "발밑을 잃고서야 돌아가는" 게 인생인 까닭이다. 그렇다면 살아가는 동안 잠시 빌렸다고 표현하는 게 적절하려나. 자신의 발밑조차 빌려 사는 주제에 남의 발밑까지 노린다

---

10 노자, 김학주 옮김, 『노자』, 을유문화사, 2005, 137쪽. 심원하여 만물의
    조종인 듯하다: 헤아릴 수 없이 깊어서 만물의 가장 근본적이고 주요한
    근거인 듯하다.

think[s] of that flower" of the spring, because he miss-es it. For the same reason, in "Itinerary" he is "eagerly looking forward to another flash of lightning, one day."

In "Tangles" there is "a flower... in love with just one single bee" and "in search of it... end[s] up "losing its scent." There is also "a bee... in love with just one single flower,/completely ignoring all the many other flowers and settling on just that one,/or sitting dumbfounded before the grave covering the fallen flower and wait-ing on and on, perhaps... end[ing] up losing its wings." Ahn Sang-hak sings of the heartrending sadness of all things, likely because he himself lost his scent and wings, like the flower and the bee he depicts. This was the place his sensibilities began to develop.

3. The Subject of Non-Doing and the Violence of Artificiality

Laozi says in the beginning of Chapter Four of Tao Te Ching, "Tao can be infused into the nature and put to use without being exhausted./It is so deep and subtle like an abyss that is the origin of all things." Here "Tao" means nature. As the substance of nature is empty, it can change every moment and embrace and nurture all things in it. As is well known, the mod-

면 이는 천만부당한 작태라 해야 한다. 그래서 시인은 타인의 발밑을 **빼앗은** 전범(戰犯)[11]에 비판을 가하는 한편 나무에게서 가르침을 구한다. "세상 누구의 발밑도 건드려서는 안 된다/ 많은 부분 나무들에게서 배우고 익힐 필요가 있다"

나무(식물)에게서 가르침을 얻으려는 자세는 「얼굴」에서도 나타난다. 제 발밑에 충실한 나무는 제 얼굴에도 충실하다. "세상 모든 나무와 풀과 꽃은/ 그 얼굴 말고는 다른 얼굴이 없는 것처럼/ 늘 그 얼굴에 그 얼굴로 살아가는 것처럼 보인다" 그렇지만 인간은 상황에 따라 얼굴을 바꾸는데, 시인은 자신을 매개로 삼아 인간의 그러한 면모를 지적한다. "어쩔 때 나는 속없는 얼굴을 굴기도 하고/ 때로는 어떤 과장된 얼굴을 만들기도" 하면서 "진짜 내 얼굴을" 숨기기 일쑤다. 인간은 왜 수 많은 얼굴을 펼쳐 보여야 하는 것일까. 작품에는 제시되지 않았으나, 아마도 무언가를 얻어내려는 욕망을 충족시키기 위함일 것이다. 그러한 판단의 근거는 「내 손이 슬퍼 보인다」에서 마련할 수 있다. 시인은 사람을 "네 발로 와서 두 손으로 살다가/ 네 발로 돌아가는" 존

11 전범(戰犯, a war criminal): 전쟁범죄자

ern subject is typically characterized as getting bigger, by constantly satisfying its desires. This is why we have to compose a subject different from this modern subject in order to learn nature's way. Accordingly, the poet presents us with a limited space, which a subject can entirely possess on his own. Let's look at the beginning of the poem "Underfoot": "The space that lies beneath my feet is mine alone./No one born at a given time on a given day/can ever stand on what lies beneath another's feet." This possession of one's underfoot is limited, as our life "starts with nothing underfoot" and "loses that [what we had underfoot during our lifetime] as it reaches its end." Thus, the space underfoot is perhaps better understood as something we momentarily borrow during our lifetime. Since we are borrowing even the space under our feet, it is absolutely unjust to take away the space under other people's feet. Therefore, the poet condemns war criminals, who took away others' space, while he looks for wisdom from trees: "We may not trespass on the space under any other person's feet./There's a need to learn and master a lot from trees."

He is also looking for wisdom from the tree and oth-

재라고 전제한다. 그리고 살아가면서 "앞발이 손이 되는 것은 대체로 소유를 위해서며", "폭력을 위해서며", "군림을 위해서"라고 질타하고 있다. 시인이 자신의 손까지도 슬프게 바라보는 까닭이 그것인바, 인간이 소유·폭력·군림을 위하여 손 내밀 때 진짜 얼굴은 숨겨야 하지 않았겠는가.

「팔레스타인 1,300인」은 자신의 발밑을 지키려다가 죽어간 이들에 관한 시편이다. 그렇기 때문에 부제는 "그들은 전사하지 않고 학살당했다"라고 제시되었다. 학살을 고발하는 여타의 문학작품이 그러하듯이, 이 시 역시 생명보다 우월한 이념·욕망 따위는 존재하지 않음을 갈파하고 있다. "오래된 신화나 낡은 종교나/ 고리대금의 자본이나 석유 냄새나는 배후나/ 거대한 제국의 그림자거나 값싼 민족주의거나/ 혹은 집 없는 설움이거나/ 사람을 죽여서 얻을 수 있는 상찬은 없다" 그런데 이러한 고발은 인위(人爲)에 내장된 폭력성과 결부됨으로써 독창성을 획득하게 된다. "인간이 인간을 제압할 수 없는 퇴화된 어금니의 역사에는/ 다수를 향한 살기를 품은 칼의 발전사가 내장되어 있다", "인간이 인간을 포획할 수 없는 퇴화된 발톱의 역사에는/ 불특정

er plants in "A Face." A tree is as loyal to its face as it is to its underfoot: "Just as there is no face other than that face,/all the trees and plants and flowers in the world,/can be seen in that face as living in that face." However, a human being changes their face according to the situation, which the poet expresses through his own behavior: "Occasionally I pretend to have a blank face,/sometimes I put on an exaggerated face. I am/inclined to hide my real face." Why should a human being wear so many faces? Although the poem does not directly answer this question, it insinuates that it's probably because of our desire to possess things. "My Hands Look Sad" supports this assumption. The poet says about human life: "Humans come four-footed, live two-handed,/then end four-footed again." He then condemns humans, saying: "Front feet becoming hands is mainly for possession,... mainly for violence," and "mainly for domination." That is why the poet says that even his own hands look sad. If humans hold out their hands for possession, violence, and domination, is it strange that they are inclined to hide their faces?

The subject of "1,300 Palestinians" is people who died trying to defend their underfoot spaces. Hence its

다수를 겨냥한 살의를 품은 총의 발전사가 암장되어 있다" 이는 무위의 편에 섰을 때 비로소 가능한 진술이다. 즉 현실 고발에서도 안상학은 그 나름의 세계관을 그대로 관철시켜 나가고 있다는 것이다.

「평화라는 이름의 칼」의 경우에는 "평화를 가장한 평화라는 이름의 칼"이 내장하고 있는 허위를 폭로하는 시편이다. 기실 '평화라는 이름의 칼'은 피로써 피를 씻어 내겠다는 논리와 태도를 상징하고 있을 터인데, 칼에 새겨진 '평화라는 이름'이 폭력이라든가 전쟁·학살과 같은 야만성을 은폐하여 하얀 여백으로 밀어내 버리는 지점에 주목할 필요가 있겠다. "소위 법 없이도 살 사람들이" 상황을 "미처 인식하기도 전에 평화라는 이름의 칼에 의해" 학살당해왔던 까닭은 그 여백을 읽어내지 못했기 때문이 아닌가. 앞서 여백을 읽기 위하여 확정된 사실(명확한 언술)을 지연시켜 나가는 시인의 태도를 분석했던 바 있다. 그러니까 이 시를 써 내려간 동력은 활자 바깥의 여백을 읽어나가고자 하는 시인의 태도에서 확보되었다고 정리해도 되겠다. 안상학의 시 세계는 무위자연의 인식을 바탕으로 구축되어 있다.

subtitle: "They did not die in battle, they were massa-cred." Like other literary works, this poem condemns this slaughter by arguing that there cannot be an ideology or desire superior to human life: "Whether it be ancient myths or old religions,/usurers' capital or backers stinking of petroleum/or the shadow cast by vast empires or cheap nationalism/or distress at be-ing homeless, there is no praise to be gained by killing people." This condemnation is unique, however, in that it points out the violence inherent in artificiality. This siding with non-doing makes it possible for the poet to make statements like: "In the history of human-ity's degenerate molars, unable to overpower/another human... is included the history/of the development of the knife, nourishing violent feelings toward the majority." and "In the history of humanity's degener-ate toes, incapable of seizing another person/... lies concealed the history/of the development of the gun, nourishing murderous intent toward the unspecified majority." In other words, Ahn Sang-hak's engage-ment in social and political reality is also based on his worldview of "non-doing naturalism."

"The Sword Named Peace" reveals the falsehood in

"the sword of peace, which simulates peace." As "the sword named peace" conceals underneath its peaceful appearance the logic and attitude that blood could be washed away only by blood, we need to pay attention to the blank margins where the name "peace" hides and pushes away barbarity like violence, war, and massacres. Haven't people, who, if left alone, could "live until they die quite without any kind of law," been "slaughtered by the sword named Peace before they ever knew about their own sword" only because they could not read what was in that margin? Above, I examined the poet's tactic of "delaying about confirmed facts [clear statements]" in order to read the margins. It seems to me that the motivation for writing this poem was secured in the poet's approach of reading the margins outside of printed letters. As such, Ahn Sang-hak's poetic world is fundamentally constructed based on the worldview of non-doing naturalism.

안상학에
대해

What They Say
About Ahn Sang-Hak

POET

서정시의 본질적 시제는 현재이다. 하지만 이는 고립된 현재가 아니라 시인의 의식상에서 과거의 많은 경험들이 동시적으로 공존하고 있거나 의미있는 패턴으로 연속되어 있는 현재이다. 따라서 현재의 대상을 상상하는 데 그치지 않고 보다 많은 과거를 집중시킴으로써 현재의 의미는 더욱 풍부하게 확산된다. 안상학은 이와 같은 서정적 시간의식에 기반을 두면서 가족에 대한 기억을 통해 인간과 인간, 혹은 인간과 자연의 관계를 맺으려는 시적 성찰을 펼치고 있다.

하상일

The essential tense of lyric poetry is the present. However, this is not an isolated present but a present where many past experiences, in the consciousness of the poet, coexist simultaneously or are linked in a meaningful pattern. Therefore, not only imagining the present object but concentrating more past contexts, the poet develops the meaning of the present more abundantly. Based on this lyrical consciousness of time, Ahn Sang-hak undertakes a poetic reflection on the relationship between person and person, or person and nature, through memories of the family.

Ha Sang-Il

안상학 시인은 세상에 대한 '미안함'을 가슴에 얹고 살아가는 사람이다. 도대체 자기 자신을 들여다볼 줄 모르는 오만하고 뻔뻔한 사람들로 가득 찬 세상에서 그는 이방인이다. 여기서 '미안함'이란 시인의 타자에 대한 윤리학적 근원이 되는 동시에 자아의 의식을 연단하는 매개 감정이다. 세상에 늘 미안하고 고마운 감정을 지닌 그이기에, 그의 눈길 닿는 곳 어디나 아름다운 힘이 꽃향기처럼 피어오른다.

김정남

미래의 어느 시간에 이루어질 일들을 기다리는 것, 미래를 기약하며 무의미한 시를 쓰는 행위는 믿음을 증명하는 일이며 자기를 학대하며 고행하는 것이다. 그 고행이야말로 가장 위대한 믿음의 증거이다. 고행을 하는 자의 눈에는 주변의 굶주린 자들의 언어와 광인의 눈빛을 통해 미래의 비밀이 가끔씩 흘러나오는 모습이 보인다. 시인은 이 비밀들을 받아 적는 자이며 안상학은 그 비밀을 과장되거나 축소하지 않은 저음의 목소리로 노래해왔다.

김성규

Ahn Sang-hak is a poet who wears the word 'sorry' toward the world written on his breast. He is a stranger in a world full of arrogant and brazen people who are incapable of looking into themselves. Here, 'sorry' serves as a mediating feeling, at the same time being the ethical source of the poet toward others and a training in awareness of self. Because he is always feeling sorry and thankful toward the world, everywhere his gaze rests a beautiful power emerges like the fragrance of a flower.

Kim Jeong-Nam

Waiting for what will happen sometime in the future, the act of writing meaningless poetry while awaiting the future, testifies to a faith, abusing and mortifying oneself. That self-mortification testifies to the greatest faith. To the eyes of one mortifying himself, occasionally through the words of the hungry and the gaze of the mad, the shape of the secrets of the future can be seen emerging. The poet is one who receives and writes those secrets, and Ahn Sang-Hak has long sung the secrets in a deep voice that neither exaggerates nor diminishes them.

Kim Sung-Gyu

K-포엣
안상학 시선

2018년 8월 13일 초판 1쇄 발행

지은이 안상학 | 옮긴이 안선재 | 펴낸이 김재범
편집장 김형욱 | 편집 강민영 | 관리 강초민, 홍희표 | 디자인 나루기획
인쇄·제책 AP프린팅 | 종이 한솔PNS
펴낸곳 (주)아시아 | 출판등록 2006년 1월 27일 제406-2006-000004호
주소 경기도 파주시 회동길 445(서울 사무소: 서울특별시 동작구 서달로 161-1 3층)
전화 02.821.5055 | 팩스 02.821.5057 | 홈페이지 www.bookasia.org
ISBN 979-11-5662-317-5 (set) | 979-11-5662-347-2 (04810)
값은 뒤표지에 있습니다.

K-Poet
Poems by Ahn Sang-Hak

Written by Ahn Sang-Hak | **Translated by** Brother Anthony of Taizé
Published by ASIA Publishers | 445, Hoedong-gil, Paju-si, Gyeonggi-do, Korea
(Seoul Office: 161-1, Seodal-ro, Dongjak-gu, Seoul, Korea)
Homepage Address www.bookasia.org | **Tel** (822).821.5055 | **Fax** (822).821.5057
ISBN 979-11-5662-317-5 (set) | 979-11-5662-347-2 (04810)
First published in Korea by ASIA Publishers 2018

This book is published with the support of the Literature Translation Institute of Korea
(LTI Korea).

K-픽션 한국 젊은 소설

최근에 발표된 단편소설 중 가장 우수하고 흥미로운 작품을 엄선하여 출간하는 〈K-픽션〉은 한국문학의 생생한 현장을 국내외 독자들과 실시간으로 공유하고자 기획되었습니다. 원작의 재미와 품격을 최대한 살린 〈K-픽션〉 시리즈는 매 계절마다 새로운 작품을 선보입니다.